Simba's Adventure

New York

It was a special day on the Pride Lands.

All the animals had traveled from afar to see the new prince, Simba.

The wise old baboon, Rafiki, held Simba high for all the animals to see.

As Simba grew older, he loved to play with his dad, Mufasa.

Mufasa was the king.

Simba and Mufasa liked to watch over the Pride Lands and talk about the animals that lived there.

One day, Simba wanted to play, but his dad was busy. "Will you play with me?" he asked his Uncle Scar.

"No, but I will tell you a great place to go—the Elephant Graveyard."

Simba and his friend, Nala, set off to the Elephant Graveyard. They were both excited—they would be leaving the Pride Lands!

"You can't go there!" Zazu squawked.
"It's very dangerous!"

Hyenas lived there! They were hungry.

Lucky for the cubs, Mufasa saved them.

The hyenas ran away as fast as they could.

That night, Mufasa and Simba went for a walk.

"Look at the stars," Mufasa told Simba. "The great kings of the past look down on us. They will be there to guide you … and so will I."

The next day, Simba saw Scar again. "Your father has a surprise for you," said Scar. "Go to the canyon."

The surprise was a trick! Scar created a stampede of wildebeests!

Mufasa tried to save his son. But Scar pushed Mufasa off a cliff!

"Run away, Simba," said Scar. "Run away and never return."

Simba thought he was to blame, so he ran far, far away. Simba ran until he collapsed.

Timon and Pumbaa found Simba.

They took him to safety.

Timon and Pumbaa took Simba to their home. They taught him about *hakuna matata*. It means "no worries."

They even taught him to eat wiggly bugs!

Simba grew up.

One day, a pretty lioness walked into the forest … Nala! The two lions were happy they had found each other.

Nala told Simba that the Pride Lands were in danger. Scar had taken over, and all the animals were scared.

Simba was afraid to go back.

That night, Simba saw his father in the sky. "Remember who you are," Mufasa told him.

Simba knew he had to go home.

Simba returned to the Pride Lands to fight Scar and reclaim his place as king.

The lions fought. Simba won!

Simba told Scar to never come back.

Simba climbed to the top of Pride Rock and roared loudly. He was king.

The Pride Lands flourished again.

THE END